HARVEY HOUSE, INC.
Publishers
Irvington-on-Hudson, N. Y. 10533

Copyright © 1969 by HARVEY HOUSE, INC. (Text)
Copyright © 1969 by BEATRICE DARWIN (Illustrations)

*All rights reserved, including
the right to reproduce this book
or portions thereof in any form.*

Library of Congress Catalog Card No.: 69-17738
Manufactured in the United States of America

Weekly Reader Children's Book Club Edition

Weekly Reader Children's Book Club presents

THE Sunflower Garden

By JANICE MAY UDRY

Illustrated by BEATRICE DARWIN

Pipsa was a little Algonkian Indian girl who lived in the eastern part of our country. She had five brothers but no sister. All the brothers except one were older than Pipsa. He was still a baby.

Pipsa's father was proud of how well her brothers could swim.

He didn't notice how well Pipsa took care of her baby brother.

Her father was proud of how well her brothers caught fish.

He didn't notice how many berries Pipsa picked.

Her father was proud of how far out into the river her brothers could throw stones.

He didn't notice how much wood Pipsa gathered for the fires.

Her father was proud of the way her brothers had learned to trap rabbits and birds.

He didn't notice the baskets Pipsa had made.

Her father was proud of the first bows made by her brothers.

He didn't notice that now Pipsa helped her mother make their clothes from deerskin.

Pipsa's father was like most Indian fathers. He taught his sons to do the things he could do, and he often praised them. He never thought of praising a little girl.

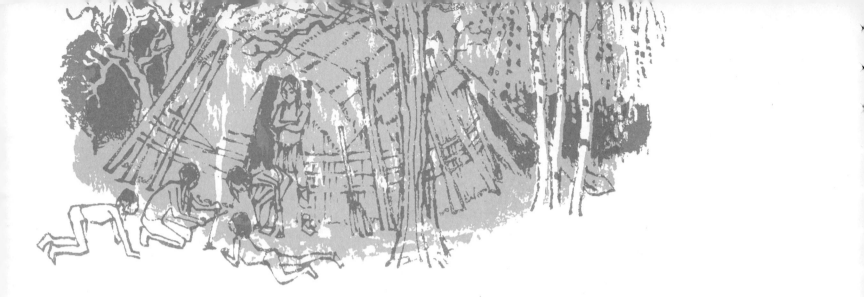

But Pipsa's mother was proud of her and sometimes said, "Well done, my little Pipsa!"

Every spring, after the redbud bloomed, Pipsa helped
her mother plant corn and beans and squash. How her
brothers loved to eat! They seldom helped with the planting or the hoeing, however.

But Pipsa's oldest brother was now allowed to take
part in the Corn Dance, which was the Indian way of
asking the Great Spirit for a good corn crop.

This year, Pipsa was eager for planting time to come. All winter she had been saving some special seeds in her private little birch-bark box. These were sunflower seeds she had gathered in the fall when her family had visited another village. There Pipsa had seen the big sunflowers growing, and she had tasted the delicious cakes that had been made from the seeds. One of the girls in the village had helped her gather leftover seeds. She told Pipsa that the seeds also made wonderful oil for the hair, and that her father sometimes crushed the dry leaves of the sunflowers and smoked them.

Now that spring was here, Pipsa planned to have a sunflower garden. No one in Pipsa's village had ever grown sunflowers. All of the work of growing them would have to be done by Pipsa herself, because her mother had all the work she could manage to do in the big corn and bean field.

While Pipsa's brothers swam and fished and practiced with their bows and arrows, Pipsa and her mother planted and hoed the vegetables. Now that Gray Squirrel, the baby brother, was over a year old, he was no longer fastened to his cradle board, and he toddled about close to his mother and sister.

The days grew warmer and warmer. Almost the only time Pipsa could work in her sunflower patch was after supper. Since the days were longer, it was light enough for her to work then. She usually had to take Gray Squirrel with her and watch that he didn't wander away into the woods.

First, Pipsa scraped away the dead leaves, the old weeds and the sticks. Then she dug and chopped the ground with a hoe and broke up all the dirt clods. She planted the sunflower seeds on an evening when she had heard her father say it would rain before morning. As she looked down at the bare, flat ground where she had planted the seeds, she wondered if the seeds were really any good. Had she planted them right? Would they grow? Pipsa waited and watched for a sign of green.

Finally, after twelve days, the first tiny green shoot appeared. In the next week Pipsa's garden became full of little plants reaching for the sun.

Every evening she chopped down any weed that had dared to invade the baby plants during the day. When the ground was dry, she watched the sky for rain clouds.

It was a good growing summer. By July, the great sunflower heads were heavy with seeds, and it would soon be time to pick them and shake out the seeds for making cakes and oil. Pipsa had to watch Gray Squirrel constantly because he wanted to play with the sunflower heads, and he kept trying to pull them down.

The other mothers and children often came to see and admire Pipsa's big bright flowers. One of the plants was truly a giant sunflower "tree," twice as tall as Pipsa.

As the seeds ripened, Pipsa found that some other creatures loved the sunflowers too.

"The birds and the mice are eating all my seeds," Pipsa told her mother sadly. She spent as much time as she could guarding the sunflowers and shooing the birds.

One evening when Pipsa was chopping weeds away from the plants and Gray Squirrel was crawling around the big leaves, Pipsa suddenly heard something frightening. She stopped and looked quickly for her baby brother. Pipsa heard a rattlesnake!

She saw the coiled creature — the biggest snake she had ever seen! It was lying in the grass waiting for the mice that came for the seeds. Now her little brother had disturbed it. The baby didn't see the snake or know what the sound meant. Pipsa put her hand to her mouth and then, grasping the hoe, she crept swiftly and silently toward the snake. She must kill it before it bit her brother. She had never been so afraid in all of her life. What if she missed? What if she only angered the snake?

With all the force she had, Pipsa whacked downward, aiming at the back of the snake's head with the hoe. Without stopping to see if she had killed it, she hit again and again. Very frightened by this time, little Gray Squirrel scrambled to his feet.

"Run, little brother, run!" cried Pipsa.

Gray Squirrel ran crying to his mother.

In a few minutes, Pipsa's mother and father and brothers came running. Gray Squirrel was still crying in his mother's arms.

Pipsa felt so weak that she had to sit down. But beside her was the dead snake. Her brothers were amazed at the size of it. They praised Pipsa for her courage, and for the first time Pipsa saw admiration in their eyes. And for the first time Pipsa's father bent over her and said, "Well done, my little daughter. You are a brave child."

Pipsa was so overcome by the fright of killing the snake and by the pride in the eyes of her brothers and her father that tears came to her eyes. But she fought them back. She didn't want to spoil this moment by crying!

Her father looked around him at the sunflower garden. It was the first time he had been there.

"What are these?" he asked her, puzzled.

"They are sunflowers, Father," she told him.

"What are they for?"

Pipsa told her father that soon they would have good little cakes from the seeds — if she could keep the birds and mice away long enough. And she told him how they could make hair oil, and how her friend's father sometimes smoked the crushed sunflower leaves in his pipe.

Pipsa's father asked her how soon they could have these things. He touched the big sunflower heads with great interest. And then he looked again at Pipsa almost as if he had never really seen her before.

He put his big hand on her head. "I am proud of you," he said.

The next day, her father told her brothers to take turns helping Pipsa guard the sunflowers until it was time to gather the seeds.

Finally, when Pipsa said that the seeds were ripe, almost everyone came to watch her gather them.

They all followed Pipsa and her family back to their home, and they watched Pipsa pound the seeds into little cakes. She gave everyone a taste. They smiled and exclaimed at the good flavor. Pipsa told them how to make oil for more beautiful hair. She gave everyone some of the seeds so that the following spring everyone in the village could grow sunflowers.

The whole village spoke proudly of the little girl who had brought a new plant and new ideas to her people. They called her the "Sunflower Girl."

As the years went by, the Indians in Pipsa's village grew more and more sunflowers, and they never forgot to give special honor to Pipsa even after she was grown and had a little girl of her own. The people often told Pipsa's little girl how her mother had grown the first sunflowers there and had given seeds to the rest of the village.

And Pipsa's brother, Gray Squirrel, never forgot that, when he was very small, she had saved his life.